HEART OF GOLD

HEART OF GOLD

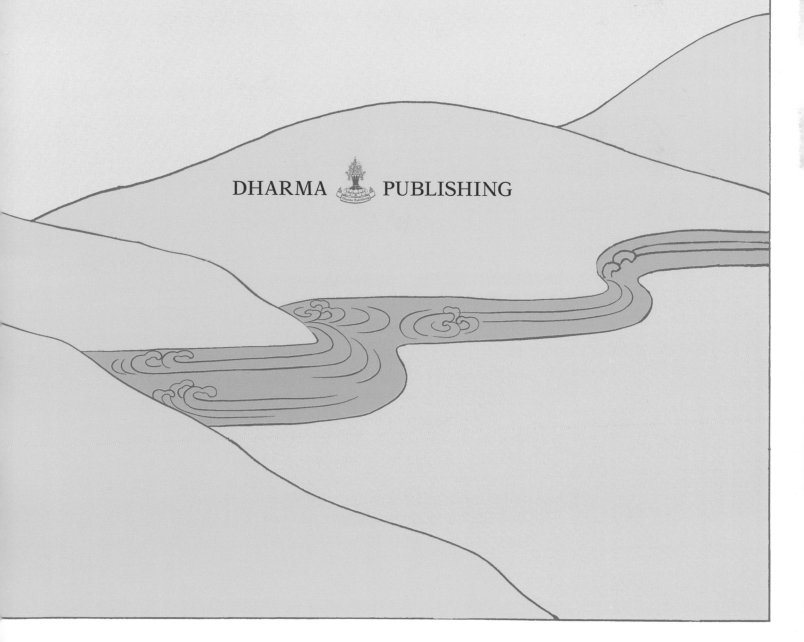

DHARMA PUBLISHING

Story adapted by Dharma Publishing editorial staff.
Illustrated by Rosalyn White.
Color design by Julia Witwer.
Printed in the USA by Dharma Press
35788 Hauser Bridge Rd., Cazadero, CA 95421

Library of Congress Cataloging in Publication Data
will be found at the end of this book.
Typeset in New Aster medium and italic.

Dedicated to

All the World's Children

The Jataka Tales

The Jataka Tales celebrate the power of action motivated by compassion, love, wisdom, and kindness. They teach that all we think and do profoundly affects the quality of our lives. Selfish words and deeds bring suffering to us and to those around us while selfless action gives rise to goodness of such power that it spreads in ever-widening circles, uplifting all forms of life.

The Jataka Tales, first related by the Buddha over two thousand years ago, bring to light his many lifetimes of positive action practiced for the sake of the world. As an embodiment of great compassion, the Awakened One reappears in many forms, in many times and places to ease the suffering of living beings. Thus these stories are filled with heroes of all kinds, each demonstrating the power of compassion and wisdom to transform any situation.

While based on traditional accounts, the stories in the Jataka Tales Series have been adapted for the children of today. May these tales inspire the positive action that will sustain the heart of goodness and the light of wisdom for the future of the world.

Tarthang Tulku   Founder, Dharma Publishing

Once in days gone by, there lived a man so wealthy that his
goods filled the many storerooms of his large mansion and spilled

out onto the lawns and walkways. Everything that could be desired or dreamed of he possessed in abundance.

What he enjoyed above all else was giving away his possessions to those less fortunate than himself. He was known far and wide as Heart of Gold, for his generosity was constant and unfailing. Every afternoon he brought baskets brimming with food and clothing into the garden and offered them to whoever was in need. He was unable to refuse any request. If someone wanted his fine books or carpets, his chariots, or even his best horses, he would give them away without a second thought.

"Possessions can cause such unhappiness," he thought. "The rich are constantly afraid of losing their wealth, while the poor are afraid of having none. What need have I of more possessions? Let my riches bring comfort to those in need."

In this way, poor people all across the land gained relief from suffering while Heart of Gold gained the joy of giving. Word spread that anyone in distress could rely upon his help, and his fame reached even to the heavens. There lived the devas, shining heavenly beings who flew high above the tallest mountains. Shakra, the powerful deva king, was fond of watching the world of men and testing their honesty and courage.

"If his heart is truly made of gold, then trials and hardship will only make it shine more brightly.

"It is too easy for such a rich man to be generous. Let him lose a little wealth, and we shall see if he doesn't become stingy!"

That very night Shakra caused the jewelry and musical instruments to disappear from the storerooms. But Heart of Gold thought nothing of it. Then the piles of carpets and curtains began to shrink

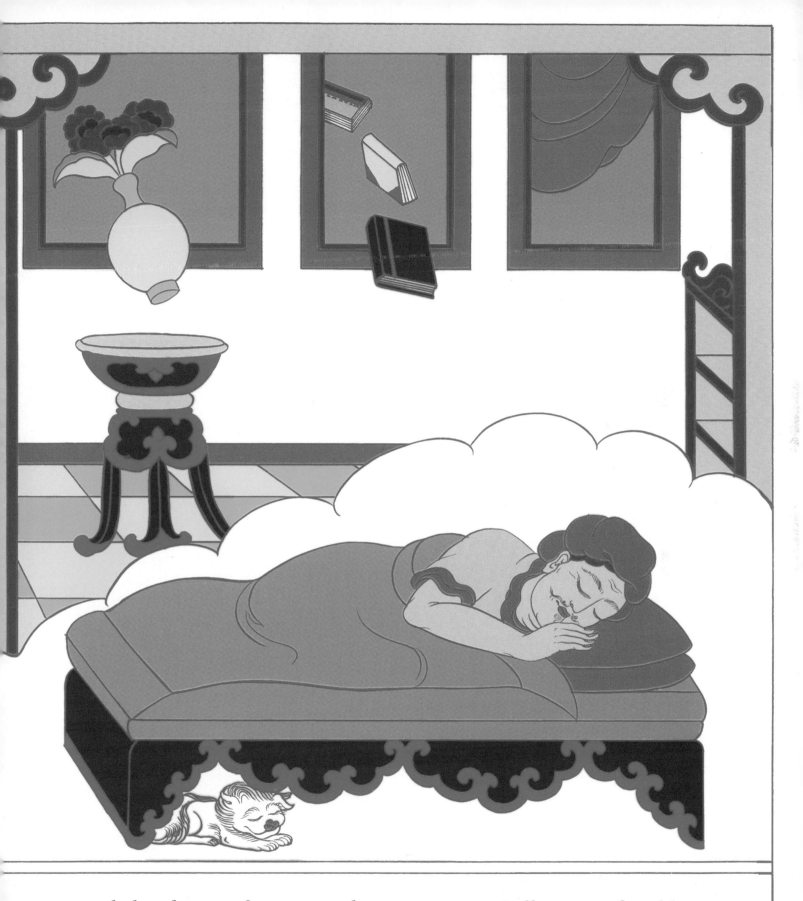

and the closets of garments became empty. Still Heart of Gold thought nothing of it. Amazed at Heart of Gold's complete lack of greed, Shakra decided upon a more difficult test.

The next morning when Heart of Gold awoke, he found his entire mansion empty as though a great wind had swept the rooms clean. Not a single piece of furniture could be found—not a suit of clothes, not even a grain of wheat. All that remained was a rope, a sickle and the night-shirt on his back.

"What a strange happening!" thought Heart of Gold. "Perhaps some needy person came secretly in the night and helped himself. If so, then my riches are well spent. But how desperate the rest of the poor folk will be when they find my house empty. Perhaps I can make use of this sickle to provide some small help."

Out into the fields he went to mow grass with the poorest folk of the village. All day long he toiled in the hot sun, thinking of the many people who possessed even less than he.

"I had not fully realized how hard is to be poor. I cannot bring myself to beg for food for it makes my heart ache to feel so helpless. Yet the poor must beg to feed their children, and the sick have no choice but to ask for help from the strong and healthy.

"Everyone wishes for happiness and everyone fears suffering. We are all alike and all together in this world. How can I ever be happy while those around me are in such pain?"

Day after day his desire to help grew stronger. Moved by this great compassion, he worked harder and faster. "If I mow enough grass, I will have something to give my poor friends!"

Whatever he earned by selling his crop, he gave happily to those in need. Boys and girls, mothers and fathers, those whom were hungry and those who were sick, those who had little and those who had nothing at all came to Heart of Gold. To each he offered a shiny golden coin before they had even spoken a word.

The merchants of the marketplace watched this poor old man who gave away all of his money and shook their heads.

"Crazy old fellow! Why don't you take care of yourself or feed your own family?"

But Heart of Gold just smiled and replied, "They are my family. Who can say we are not all related? In some other time and some other place, this poor hungry lady might have been my own mother."

But the king of the devas was not yet finished with his test. Wrapped in his magical cloak of clouds so that none but Heart of Gold could see him, he appeared in the sky and spoke these clever words:

"Oh foolish man! I urge you now to restrain your love of giving! Through restraint you can increase your wealth. Once you have recovered your riches, you will be able to give more to others. There is nothing wrong in not giving when you truly have nothing to give."

Heart of Gold exclaimed, "Shakra, there is no time for what you suggest. See the suffering all around us! If a poor man is hungry and asks for my help today, I would not have him wait until my fortunes increase. Anyone who desires to protect beings will give all that he can, whenever it is needed. I will not change my practice of charity, for it brings great benefits to others and great joy to me."

At last Shakra was completely convinced. "Now I know your inner nature is pure and strong. How your noble heart shines like the sun, for you have removed the dark clouds of selfish feelings.

Whether rich or poor, your heart of gold is constant and true. I can no more move you than a breath of wind could move a mountain. Come, noble sir, I have something to confess to you."

With a wave of his hand, Shakra restored all the fine possessions to the mansion, returning every last jewel to the treasure chests and every single grain of wheat to the pantries.

"It was I who made your wealth disappear. Forgive me, and henceforth shower your gifts as freely as thunderclouds release the rain."

Heart of Gold continued to perfect his practice of generosity until his love for others included every single person in the whole world. His story shows that generosity is indeed the way to happiness.

If you possess a generous heart, your joy will be deep and true. The happiness you give to others will always return to you!

The Jataka Tales Series

Library of Congress Cataloging in Publication Data

Heart of Gold

(Jataka tales series)

Summary: Heart of Gold continues to treat the poor of the world with generosity and charity, even after a sky spirit tests him by removing all his wealth.

1. Jataka stories, English [1. Jataka stories]

I. White, Rosalyn, ill. II.Series.

BQ1462.E5H43 1989   294.3'823   88-33444

ISBN 10   0-89800-193-5

ISBN 13   978-0-89800-193-8